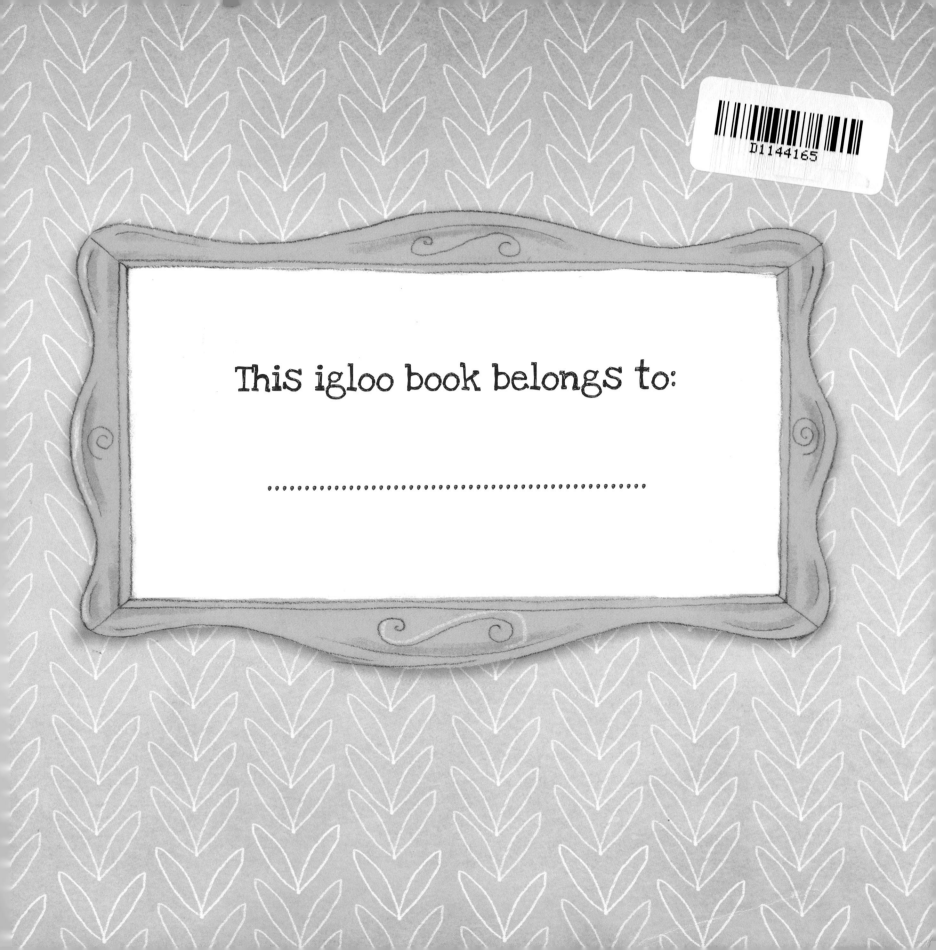

This igloo book belongs to:

....

igloobooks

Published in 2018
by Igloo Books Ltd
Cottage Farm
Sywell
NN6 0BJ
www.igloobooks.com

STI002 0618
2 4 6 8 10 9 7 5 3
ISBN 978-1-78670-561-7

Written by Melanie Joyce
Illustrated by Lizzie Walkley

Cover designed by Nicholas Gage
Interiors designed by Amy Bradford
Edited by Natalia Boileau

Printed and manufactured in Italy

WHEN I GROW UP

igloobooks

When I grow up, I'll be **famous**.
I'll be a mega star.

I'll wear a sparkly silver costume
and play an electric **guitar**.

When I grow up, I'll be **royal**.
Maybe I'll get to be Queen.

I'll have more crowns and tiaras than anyone's **ever** seen.

I'll be an **inventor** when I grow up.
What I make will be a surprise.

Everyone will be so **amazed,**
they won't believe their eyes.

I'll be a **pirate** when I grow up.
I'll join a pirate crew.

We'll look for clues on our special map,
and dig up **treasure,** too.

I'll be a **magician** when I grow up.
I'll pull rabbits out of a hat.

When I grow up, I'll be an **astronaut.**
I'll fly a rocket up to Mars.

I'll **whizz** around the moon,
and bring back lots of stars.

I'll be a **ballerina** when I grow up,
with a tutu and pink ballet shoes.

I'll leap across the stage,
and get lots of **"Aahs!"** and **"Oohs!"**

When I grow up, I'll visit places
that **no one** has ever been.

When I come back, I'll tell stories
about the **amazing** things I've seen.

I'll be an **explorer** when I grow up,
with an enormous magnifying glass.

I'll search for strange new creatures,
that might be **lurking** in the grass.

I'm sure that when I grow up,
there will be **lots** of things I can be.

But I won't think about that right now,
because we've got spaghetti for tea.